A Sticky Situation

Written by **Rachel Dennett**
Illustrated by **Niall Harding**

Endpapers illustrated by **Robin Davies**
Edited by **Emily Stead**

Published in Great Britain in 2017
by Geech Limited

A catalogue record for this book is available from the British Library.

1 3 5 7 9 10 8 6 4 2
Printed in Great Britain
www.five-a-dale.com

At Five-a-Dale Primary School, the day of the summer fair had arrived at last! Pip Apple, one of the Krunchitz, had been looking forward to this day all year.

Pip put on his new trainers. He wanted to get to the fair as quickly as he could!

"I hope there's a bouncy castle," Pip said to his mum. "It's definitely my favourite."

"Here's some pocket money!" Mrs Apple smiled, sliding a few coins into Pip's hand. "Spend it wisely."

"Thanks, Mum!" Pip said.

He waved goodbye and skipped down the lane, full of excitement at the thought of all the rides and stalls at the fair. All his friends would be there, too.

As Pip jogged into Vitamin Crescent, he could hear the hustle and bustle of the fair.

Pip loved to run. It helped keep him fit and healthy. He was about to speed up, when he noticed that his lace had come undone.

He bent down to tie it up. "The only trip I want to take is to the fair!" said Pip.

Just then, Pip heard a **'Beep! Beep!'** behind him. It was Floss in her candy van.

"Hop in the back," called Floss. "Why bother walking to the fair when you can drive?"

Pip frowned. Dodgitz never walked anywhere – they were far too lazy!

He thought for a moment, then he smiled. "Just this once," Pip called back. He didn't want to miss anything at the fair.

Pip couldn't believe his eyes as he climbed into the back of the van. It was packed with sweets! There were bags of brandy snaps and cinder toffee, clouds of candy floss, sticks of rock and rainbow lollipops. His mouth began to water.

"What are you going to do with all these sweets, Floss?" Pip called.

"They're to sell to the children at the fair," Floss shouted proudly.

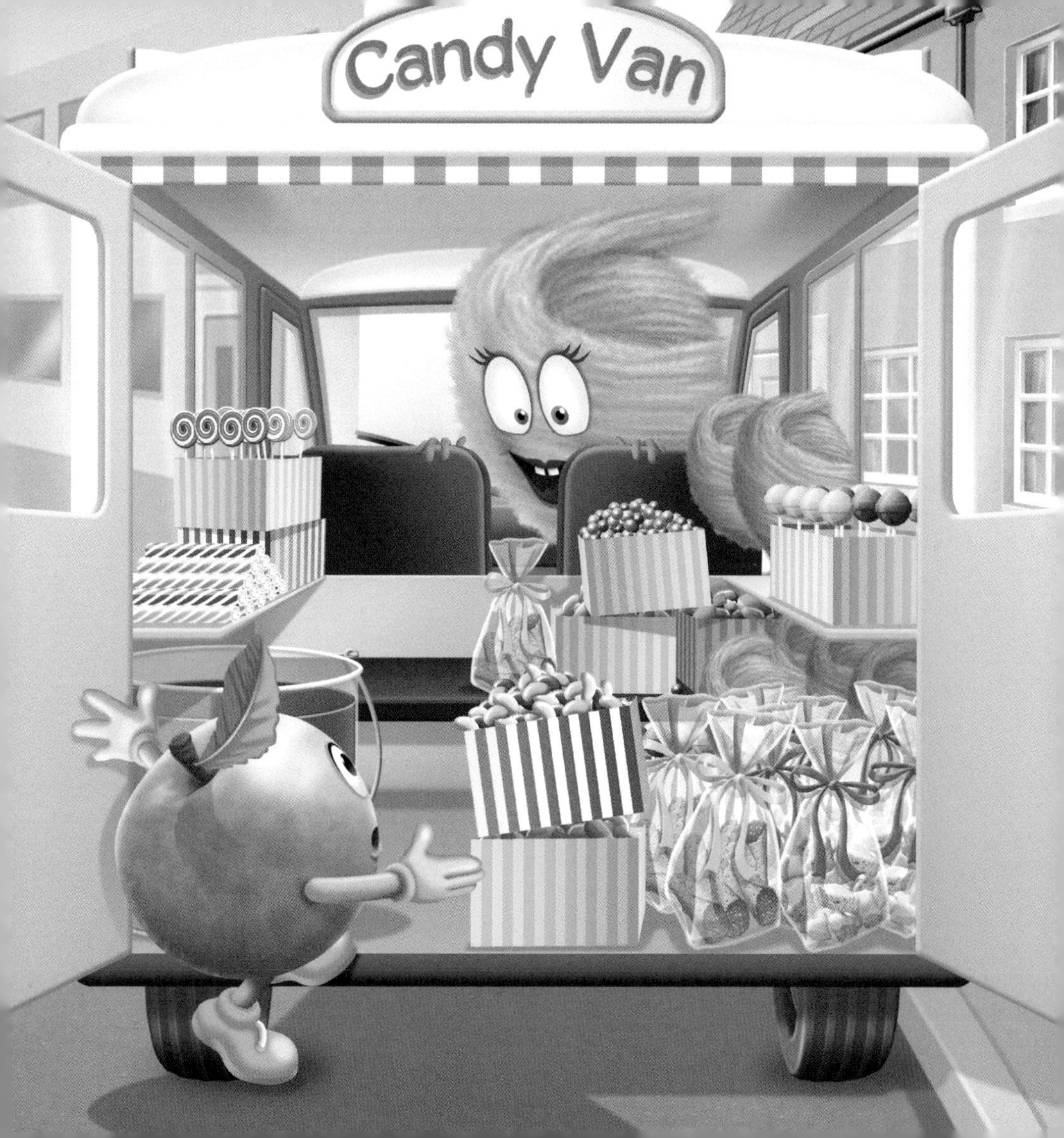
Candy Van

Pip looked at the sweets again. "But these are so bad for our teeth and bodies," he called.

"They taste good to me!" Floss shrugged.

Pip pointed to a tub filled with a sticky red liquid. "What's that?" he asked.

"That's my toffee-apple syrup. I cover old apples in it and no one can tell the difference!" Floss sniggered.

Pip frowned. **Fresh** fruit was so much more healthy!

Floss was still busy chatting and didn't notice a speedbump in the road ahead. **BASH!**

The van swayed, sending Pip flying. He landed head first in the toffee-apple sauce! **SPLAT!**

"Hmmphff!" Pip tried to call for help, but he couldn't move. The sugary syrup had him well and truly stuck!

Soon, the van arrived at Five-a-Dale Primary School. Floss hopped down from the cab.

But when she opened the back of the van to unload the sweets, Pip had disappeared... or so Floss thought!

"He must have gone to find his friends," she said to herself.

Pip was left alone. What a sticky situation!

It wasn't until later, when Floss came to unload the last of the sweets, that she discovered her friend had turned into a toffee apple!

As she reached for a box of lollipops, a sticky red blob stared back at Floss.

"**Eeek!**" shrieked Floss. "P-P-Pip, is that **you**?"

From beneath the toffee, Pip blinked twice. He felt very sorry for himself.

The syrup had set hard. Floss had to chip away and scrub for ages to free her friend. Then at last, Pip felt clean and fresh and back to normal. He never wanted to see another toffee apple again!

"This will cheer you up," said Floss, waving an enormous lollipop. "You can have it for free!"

"No thanks, Floss," Pip replied. "I'm going to steer clear of sugary things for a while!"

Pip helped Floss carry the last boxes of apples to her stall. But he was puzzled. "Floss, why do you want to turn something that's so good for people into something bad?" he asked.

"What's so great about apples?" said Floss.

"Well," Pip began. "Apples can help our bodies stay healthy in all sorts of ways..."

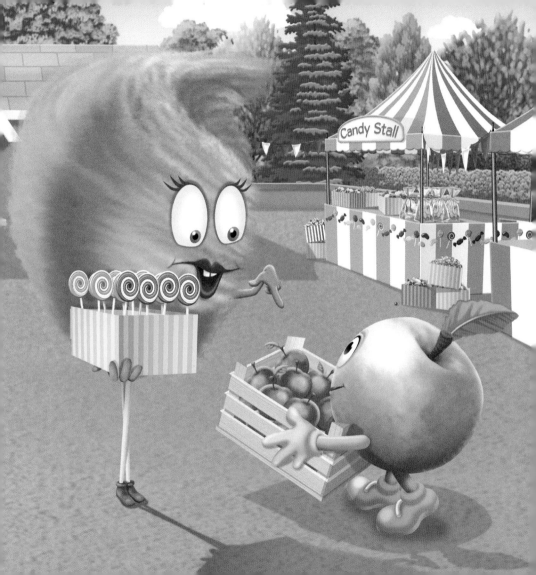

"They are full of fibre to keep our tummies working properly and their vitamins and minerals help keep us feeling well. Crunchy apples make a much better snack than sweets," Pip told his friend.

"Wow! Apples are amazing!" Floss gasped.

As they reached Floss's stall, Pip smiled. "I've had a great idea for you to sell your apples, just as they are," he said.

Together, Pip and Floss filled a large tub with water and floated the apples on top.

Floss's apple-bobbing stall was the busiest stall of all! Everyone queued to try to catch an apple. Even some of the Dodgitz had a turn!

"Thanks for your help, Pip," Floss said, at the end of the day. "Apples really **are** amazing!"

Talk about the story

What did you learn reading the story?

There are thousands of different sorts of apples, so you're bound to find one you like!

How do you think Pip felt when he was covered in toffee?

First Day at School

A Sticky Situation

More Five-a-Dale stories are coming soon!

Meanwhile, you can join in the fun with
all the Five-a-Dale friends at
www.five-a-dale.com

Stay safe online:
Five-a-Dale is not responsible for
content hosted by third parties.

Printed in Great Britain
by Amazon